Lois Lenski's
BIG BIG BOOK
of MR. SMALL

ABOUT THE AUTHOR

Lois Lenski was born in Springfield, Ohio, in 1893, and was educated at Ohio State University and the Westminster School of Art in London. She began writing and illustrating books for children in 1927 and, in a career that spanned nearly half a century, she published more than fifty titles, among them *Phebe Fairchild, Indian Captive, Bayou Suzette, Judy's Journey, Cotton in My Sack, Texas Tomboy, Flood Friday, Blue Ridge Billy,* and numerous others that are still perennial favorites of young readers everywhere. In 1946 Lois Lenski received the prestigious Newbery Medal for *Strawberry Girl* and she was the recipient of several other awards for children's books, as well. Lois Lenski died in 1974.

For the children of the children
who first loved Mr. Small

Lois Lenski's
BIG BIG BOOK
of MR. SMALL

DERRYDALE BOOKS
New York

Library of Congress Cataloging in Publication Data

Lenski, Lois, 1893–1974
Lois Lenski's big big book of Mr. Small.

"Previously published as two separate collections entitled The big book of Mr. Small and More Mr. Small"—P.
Contents: Policeman Small—Cowboy Small—The little farm—[etc.]
1. Children's stories, American. I. Title.
PZ7.L54Bg 1985 [E] 84-21404
ISBN: 0-517-463075

hgfedc

The stories in this book appear in the following order:

POLICEMAN SMALL

Oh, Do You Know Policeman Small?

WORDS BY LOIS LENSKI
MUSIC BY CLYDE ROBERT BULLA

Policeman Small is a traffic cop.
He stands at the street crossing.
He wears white gloves. He tells the cars
when to go and stop.

It is six o'clock in the morning.
Here comes the milk delivery truck.
    "Hello, Joe!" calls Policeman Small.
"Has everybody got milk for breakfast?"
    "Yes!" says Joe.

It is eight-thirty.

Here come the school children walking to school.

Policeman Small holds up his hand. The children cross the street.

They say, "Hello, Policeman Small!"

It is nine o'clock.

Here comes a farmer in a truck. He has a load of vegetables for the grocery store. He waves to Policeman Small.

It is ten o'clock.

Here comes a sports car very fast.

It comes faster and faster. It is speeding.

Policeman Small blows his whistle very loud. He holds up his hand.

The car stops. Policeman Small
runs up. "No speeding here, sir!"
he says. "25 miles an hour in town!"
"Sorry!" says the young man.
He drives on.

It is ten-thirty.

A siren sounds. It goes on and on. Here comes an ambulance. It is going to the hospital. Somebody is sick.

Policeman Small clears the street. The ambulance goes whizzing by.

It is eleven o'clock. Here comes a circus parade. The band is playing. Policeman Small is on his motorcycle. He rides in front to lead the way.

It is eleven-thirty.

The parade is over. Policeman Small
shoos the people back to the sidewalk.
A little boy is lost. He cries and cries.

Policeman Small finds his mother
for him.

It is twelve o'clock.

Here comes another farm truck. It has milk cans in the back. It goes rattledy-bang! A milk can falls off. The milk spills on the street.

Tweet-tweet-tweet! Policeman Small blows his whistle.

The farmer stops his truck.

"Sorry!" he says.

"Too bad!" says Policeman Small.

They pick up the milk can and put it
on the truck. The truck goes on to the dairy.

Policeman Small holds up his hand.
Two cats are licking up the spilled milk.
They are hungry. The cars must wait.

Twelve-thirty. It is lunch time.
Policeman Small goes to a drug store.
He eats two sandwiches. He has ice
cream and coffee. He takes a little rest.

Now it is afternoon. Traffic is heavy.
Policeman Small brings his Stop-Go sign.
Cars and trucks come rolling by.
Big cars and little cars. Big trucks and
little trucks. A boy on a bicycle.
Policeman Small turns on "Go."
They all go.

It is one-thirty.

Policeman Small turns on "Stop."
The cars stop. All the people cross. A little
dog stops in the middle of the street.

Policeman Small picks him up. He puts
him on the sidewalk. Now he is safe.

The cars can go again.

It is two o'clock.

Bang, bangety, bump! A big truck bumps into the back of a little car.

Policeman Small runs over.

"Hey!" he calls. "Pull up by the curb."

"His brakes are not good!" says the man
in the little car.

"He stopped too soon!" says the man
in the truck.

Policeman Small writes down their names
and license numbers. He gives them tickets.
He sends them to the police station to talk it over.

It is three o'clock.

The two men come out of the police station.

"We have settled it. He will pay the damage and fix his brakes," says the man in the little car.

"Good!" says Policeman Small.

The men drive off.

It is four o'clock.

R-r-r-r-r-r! A school bus
goes rolling by. It is full of children.
They are going home from school.

They wave to Policeman Small.

It is five o'clock.

A siren sounds. It goes on and on.

Policeman Small blows his whistle three times. He holds out both his arms. He clears the street.

A fire engine goes whizzing by. It is going to a fire. All the people look.

Now it is gone.

Policeman Small turns on "Go."

The cars can go again. They are all going home. It is getting late.

It is six o'clock.

"Whew!" says Policeman Small.

'Big day today! Now I can go home!"

He picks up his Stop-Go sign and goes.

His day is over.

*And that's all
about
Policeman Small!*

bedroll—blankets rolled up
bit—metal bar in horse's mouth
bridle—straps around horse's head, with bit and reins
brand—a mark
bronco—wild horse, not used to a rider
bucking—kicking, with head between front legs
bunk—bed
bunkhouse—house for cowboys' beds
chaps—overalls of leather, open at the back
chuckwagon—wagon that carries food and bedrolls
                  for cowboys
corral—a fenced-in yard for cows or horses
curries—scrapes the horse's hide with a currycomb
dismounts—gets down
girth—strap around the body of the horse,
             to hold the saddle in place
mounts—gets up
ranch—a large farm with grass for cows
range—open place where cows eat grass
reins—straps used to drive a horse
saddle—seat for rider, made of leather
stirrup—loop at end of strap hung from saddle,
               to hold foot of rider

Cowboy Small

"Hi, there!"
calls
Cowboy Small.

Cowboy Small
has a horse.
His name is Cactus.
He keeps him in the barn
at Bar S Ranch.

Cowboy Small
takes good care
of Cactus.
He brushes him and curries him.

He feeds him
oats and hay.

He gives him water
to drink.

Cowboy Small
puts the saddle on.
He pulls the girth tight.

"Whoa, Cactus!"

Cowboy Small
puts his left foot
in the stirrup
and mounts.

"Giddap, Cactus!"

Cowboy Small rides out
on the range.
Cloppety, cloppety, clop!

"Whoa, Cactus!"

Cowboy Small
dismounts.
He fixes the fence.

Cowboy Small makes camp
for the night.
He cooks supper and eats it.
Oh, how good it tastes!

Cowboy Small rolls up
in his bedroll.
He goes to sleep
under the stars.

Next morning,
Cowboy Small rides in the Bar S roundup.

The cowboys round up all the cows.
"Yip-pee! Yip-pee! Yip-pee!"

"Come and get it!"
calls the cook at noon.

Cowboy Small
eats at the chuckwagon
with the cowboys.
They have beef,
red beans and coffee.

"Yip-pee!
Ride 'em, cowboy!"

Cowboy Small
ropes a calf
in the corral.

Cowboy Small helps
with the branding.
The calves are marked
with the Bar S brand:

S̄

Cowboy Small
turns the cows back
on the range.

At night,
Cowboy Small
plays his guitar
and sings:

*"Home . . .
    home on the range . . ."*

He goes to sleep
in the bunkhouse.

Next day,
Cowboy Small
rides a bucking bronco.

"Yip-pee! —Yip-pee!
Ride 'em, cowboy!"

Ker-plop!

Cowboy Small
hits
    the
        dust!

But—
    he's a pretty good cowboy,
        after all!
    Cactus is waiting,
                so—

"Giddap, Cactus!"

Cowboy Small
rides
again!

The
LITTLE FARM

For Nina and Toni

The Little Farm

Farmer Small lives
on a farm.
He gets up early
in the morning.

He goes to the barn
to feed the animals.
They are all very
hungry.

He milks the cows.

He strains the milk
into the milk cans.
He sets them in the
milk cooler.

Farmer Small takes
the cows to pasture.

Farmer Small leaves
the cans of milk
on the milkstand.
The milk truck takes them
to the dairy.

Farmer Small feeds
the pigs.
They are
very hungry!

So are
the chickens,
the ducks
and
the turkeys!

At noon,
Farmer Small goes
   to the mailbox
   and gets his mail.

Farmer Small
has a tractor
to help him
with his work.

In the spring,
Farmer Small plows
the field
with his tractor.

He harrows
the field
with his tractor.

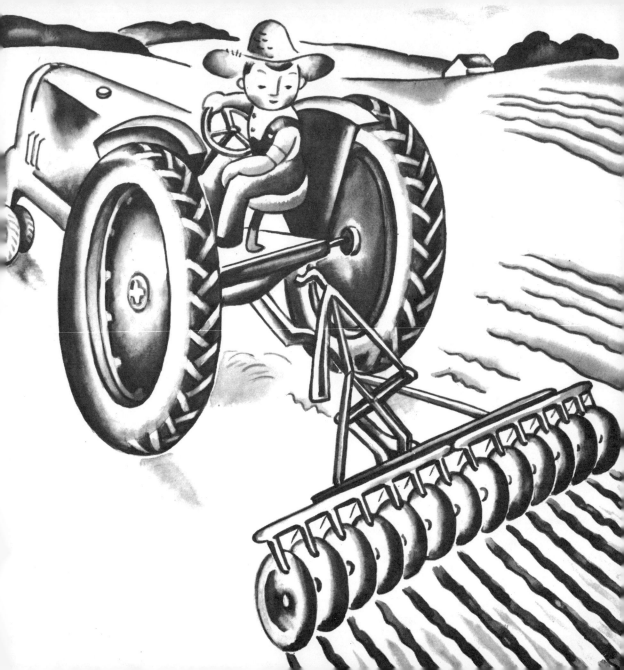

In the summer,
Farmer Small
cuts his hay
with his tractor.

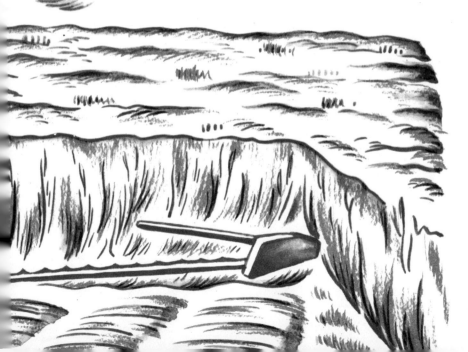

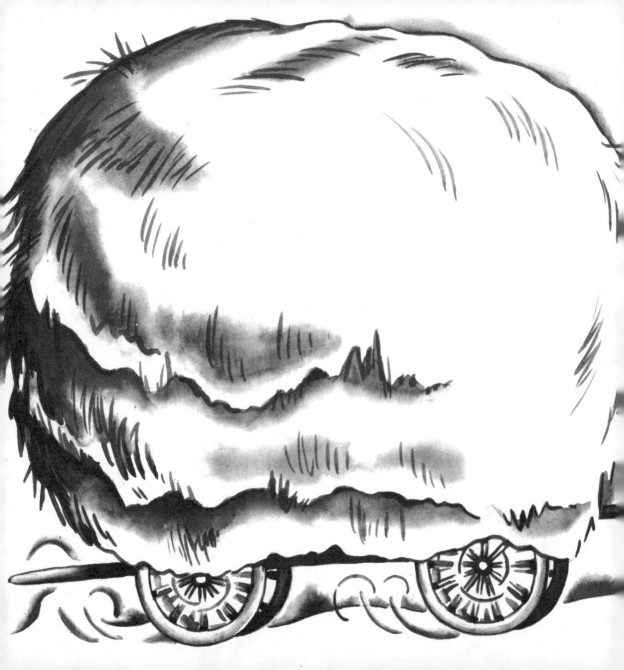

He hauls the loads of hay
to the barn.

In the fall,
Farmer Small
    picks apples
    in his orchard.

He hauls them
in the trailer
behind the tractor.

He sells them
at his
roadside stand.

In the winter,
Farmer Small
    chops his firewood.

He hauls the wood
on his bobsled
with his team.

Each day,
when evening comes,
Farmer Small gathers
the eggs.

He brings the cows
in from the pasture
and milks them.

Then
he goes into the house
to eat his supper—
and the sun goes down.

And
that's all—
about
Farmer Small!

The
LITTLE AUTO

The Little Auto

Mr. Small has a little Auto. It is red and shiny. He likes to look at it.

Mr. Small keeps
the little Auto in
the garage at the
end of the
driveway.

Mr. Small has
overalls on. He
is oiling the
little Auto

The little Auto has
rubber tires. Mr.
Small is pumping
them up.

The little Auto
has a radiator.
Mr. Small is fill-
ing it with water.

It is a fine day.
Mr. Small is going
for a drive. He steps
on the starter.
The engine begins
to hum.

The little Auto backs
out of the garage.
It goes chug-chug
down the
driveway.

The little Auto goes
down the road. Mr.
Small toots the horn,
"Beep, beep!" He
scares the ducks
and chickens.

A small dog follows
the little Auto,
but is soon left
    far behind.

The little Auto
is going fast. It
passes a horse
and buggy.

The little Auto
goes
UP HILL

and
the little Auto
goes DOWN
HILL!

The little Auto
comes to town.
Mr. Small drives
down the right
side of the street.

The little Auto
comes to a STOP-GO
sign, and waits for
the policeman to
turn it.

The little Auto
goes down
  MAIN STREET.

The little Auto
stops at a Filling
Station. Mr. Small
buys five gallons
of gas.

The little Auto
catches up with a
Trolley Car.   It
waits for the peo-
ple to get off.

Mr. Small parks
the little Auto in
front of a store.
He is going in to
buy a newspaper.

The little Auto
starts for home.
It comes to a red
light and waits
for it to turn
green.

On the way home
it begins to rain.
Mr. Small has to
put the top up so
he won't get wet.

"Pop!"
Mr. Small has a
flat tire!

Mr. Small jacks
the little Auto up.
He puts on the
spare tire.   And
then the sun
      comes out!

Soon the little
Auto is back in the
garage. After it is
washed and polished
it shines like new.

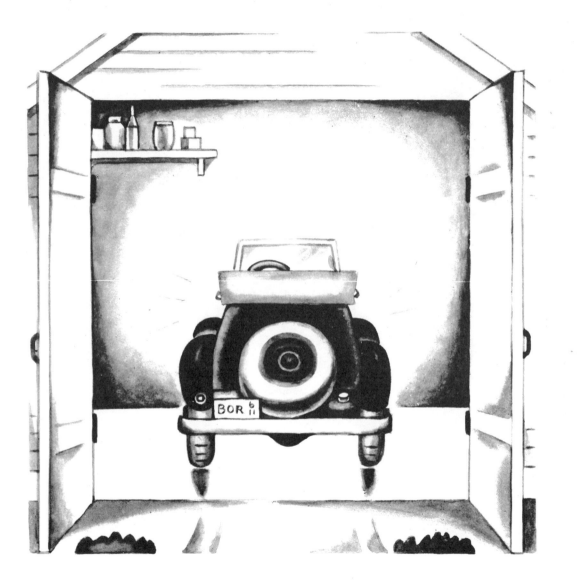

and
  that's all!

The
LITTLE
SAIL BOAT

The Little Sail-Boat

Captain Small has a
sail-boat. He keeps it
anchored off-shore.

It is a fine day. Captain Small gets into his row-boat and rows out. He is taking his fishing-line, lunch basket and small dog, Tinker, with him.

Captain Small takes
in the oars and makes
the row-boat fast to
the mooring.

He gets aboard
the sail-boat and hoists
the sail.

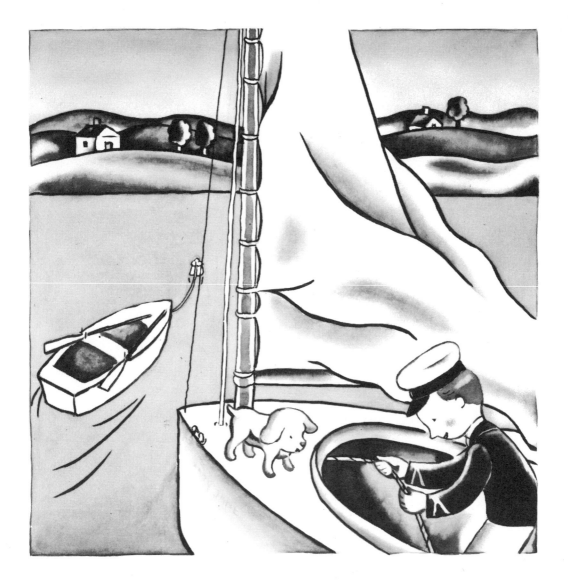

He drops the mooring and the boat starts to move. Tinker sits in the bow. He likes to sail, too.

Sitting in the stern, Captain Small takes the tiller and puts the boat before the wind. He sails for some distance.

He decides to jibe ~to turn toward the shore. He pulls the tiller and ducks his head to let the sail swing over to the other side.

Now he is sitting with his back to the wind,- or, to windward.

He comes into a quiet little cove where the fishing is good.   He drops the anchor and lowers sail.

Captain Small gets out
his fishing-line and puts
bait on the hook. He throws
it away from the boat; the
cork floats on the water.
Now he is waiting for a
nibble!

He waits...and waits...
but all the fish seem to
be somewhere else. The
sun is hot...and Captain
Small grows tired of
waiting. He falls asleep...

Suddenly a sharp tug on
the line wakes him up.
He pulls it in and finds
a big, fat fish wiggling
on the hook. He is so
excited that...

He tumbles overboard!
Tinker barks! But never
mind! The water is so
nice and cool, he decides
to enjoy a good swim.

When he climbs back on
deck, he feels very hungry,
so he and Tinker eat their
lunch. The sun soon dries
his clothes.

Captain Small rests awhile and then it is time to start for home.   He hoists the sail and raises anchor.

On the way back, he
sails against the wind
in a zigzag course.

A speed-boat roars by. The waves rock the sail-boat and make the sails flap. Tinker does not like it.

The sky grows dark. The waves splash over the bow. The wind blows hard. The boat heels over and almost upsets. But brave Captain Small brings it up into the wind. Then he sails safely into the bay.

Captain Small makes
the sail-boat fast to the
mooring. He and Tinker get
into the row-boat. He rows
as fast as he can to the dock.

Just as they climb out, the downpour comes. They are waiting in the boat-house until it is over.

After the storm,
Captain Small and Tinker
drive home in
the little Auto!

That night, Captain Small
has fish for supper. Tinker
has two dog biscuits.
Are they good?
                    Oh my!

Yes,
that's all!

The
LITTLE
AIRPLANE

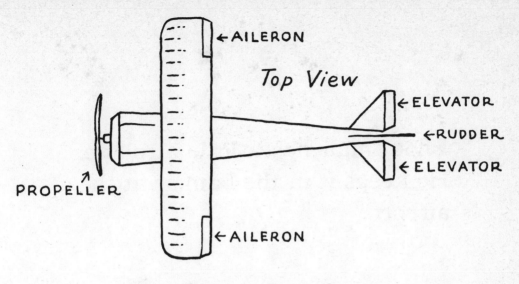

← AILERON

Top View

← ELEVATOR

←RUDDER

← ELEVATOR

PROPELLER

← AILERON

The Little Airplane

Pilot Small has a little airplane. He keeps it in the hangar at the airport.

It is a fine, sunny day. Pilot Small and the mechanic roll the airplane out of the hangar. Pilot Small decides to go up. They look the motor over carefully. They fill the tanks with gas.

All is ready for the take-off. Pilot Small climbs into the cockpit and sits down. He fastens his safety belt. He looks round on all sides to make sure the field is clear.

Pilot Small pumps the throttle a few times to prime the engine. The mechanic winds the propeller until the gas gets into the motor. Then he calls, "Contact!" Pilot Small turns on the switch and answers, "Contact!" The mechanic pulls the propeller through and it starts whizzing. The engine starts with a loud roar.

Pilot Small races the engine a few times. It roars loudly. He releases the brake. He looks at the wind indicator to see which way the wind is blowing. He taxies to the end of the field, in order to bring the plane round into the wind. He keeps the stick back to raise the elevators. The wind pressure on them keeps the plane down.

Now he is ready to take off. The motor is warmed up. He allows the stick to go forward gradually, until the tail-skid lifts. When flying speed is reached, he pulls back gently on the stick. This raises the elevators and lifts the plane off the ground. The plane climbs steeply into the wind.

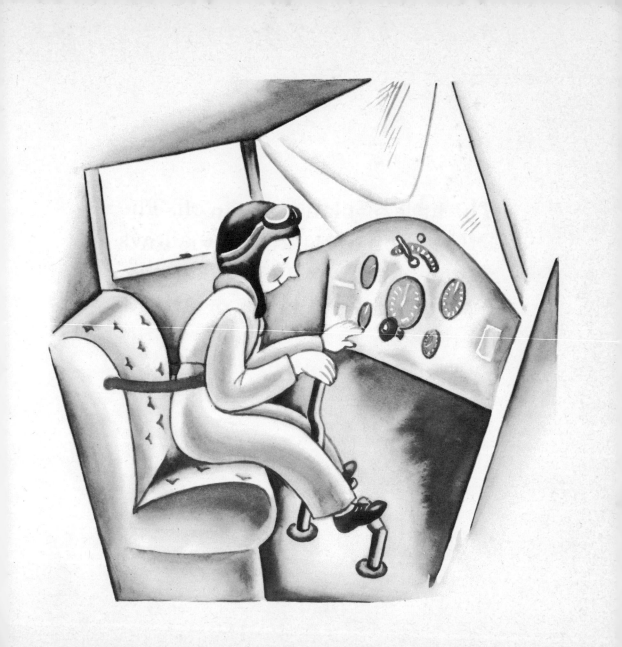

The little airplane rises in the air. Pilot Small looks down and watches the ground slip away beneath him. He keeps one hand on the gas.

Up and up the little airplane goes until it reaches a height of 2000 feet. Pilot Small pushes the stick half-way forward, into neutral, to level off. The plane flies along smoothly.

Pilot Small decides to make a right turn. He pushes the stick to the right. This lowers the aileron on the left wing and raises the aileron on the right wing. At the same time, he presses on the rudder bar with his right foot, turning the rudder to the right. The plane *banks* as it turns to the right. Then he straightens the rudder and puts the stick back to neutral, to come out of the turn. He continues on a straight course.

The little airplane flies over a large lake. It hits the air pocket and drops thirty feet. The jolt gives Pilot Small an empty feeling in his stomach, but he does not mind. He flies low over the lake. He peeps out and sees his little Sail Boat rocking at anchor beneath him. He speeds up his motor and the little airplane climbs again.

The little airplane flies over a town. Pilot Small sees the people walking about like little ants on the streets below.

The little airplane climbs higher and higher. It climbs up through open holes in the clouds toward the blue sky above. It flies above the clouds. Pilot Small likes this the best of all! He sees the clouds like layers and layers of cotton beneath him. It is a very beautiful sight!

The little airplane glides down through the clouds. It sinks gently through the foggy, dry mist. Now it is below the clouds. Pilot Small sees the ground appear again beneath him.

Pilot Small decides to do a loop. He pushes the throttle wide open to gain speed. He puts the stick forward to put the nose down. He pulls back on the stick gradually. The little airplane dives first, then climbs up sharply, turns over and comes back to its first position. Pilot Small is pushed down into his seat. He gasps for breath, then gives a chuckle. He feels very proud of himself. He does another loop just for fun!

Just then the engine begins to sputter. Chuck-a, chuck-a, chuck-a-a - - It stops dead. The gas line is clogged. The little airplane glides and begins to sink slowly. Pilot Small looks worried.

Pilot Small looks for a safe landing place. He sees an open field at the edge of a dense forest. Perhaps it is a swamp. Perhaps it is full of rocks and stones. He hopes not for he will have to make a forced landing.

The little airplane glides to the ground. It lands safely in a grassy field. Pilot Small climbs out of the cockpit. He takes tools from his tool box. He fixes the gas line and his motor begins to hum once more. What a relief! Pilot Small smiles broadly. He takes off again. Away goes the little airplane!

It is growing late. Pilot Small banks again to return. He flies back to the airport. He flies low over his home. He sees his fields, his house and his garage. Circling above the airport, he sees his little Auto waiting for him beside the hangar.

The flight is over. Pilot Small decides to land. He circles to the right of the field. He looks at the wind indicator to see which way the wind is blowing. He decides on a point on the field which he wishes to hit and keeps his eye on it. He throttles his motor down to lose speed. He glides down against the wind.

As he comes close to the ground, he pulls the stick back to level off. The little airplane drops to the ground. It makes a perfect three-point landing. The two wheels and the tail-skid hit the ground at the same moment.

Pilot Small sets one brake and turns round. He taxies, *bumpety-bump*, to the hangar. He shuts off the motor. The propeller stops. He opens the door of the cockpit and steps out.

Pilot Small and the mechanic roll the little airplane into the hangar. Pilot Small jumps into his little Auto and drives off!

And that's all

about Pilot Small!